Ouroboros Thoughts

- A POETRY COLLECTION -

BY

C. L. ADAMS

This collection of poetry is a work of fiction. Names, characters, places and incidents are either the product of the author's imagination or are used fictitiously or in reference. Any resemblance to persons living or dead, or locales are purely coincidental.

Copyright © 2023 C. L. Adams

Front & Rear Cover created using Canva. Interior images manipulated from public domain sources such as from Google Images, Unsplash and Flikr by C. L. Adams. Editing program used was Paint.NET.

All rights reserved. No parts of this collection, including the cover, may be reproduced or used in any manner without written permission of the copyright owners, except for the use of quotations in book reviews.

All uses of the title "Ouroboros Thoughts" as depicted in this instance are included within the copyright.

Ouroboros Thoughts first published 2023 via KDP.

For Dave,

who taught me not to be afraid to share all that I kept inside for so long.

Contents

Foreword

Part 1:

Oh, The Sea

This too, I Leave

Stargazing

Static

Filled with Void

Exhausted

Oasis

Contents (cont.)

Part 2:

15.06.14

01.11.14

10.11.14

22.03.15

20.06.15

23.03.16

10.03.17

27.06.18

10.01.19

Contents (cont.)

Part 3:

Ember

Vengeance

Mortar

Desiderium

Fractured

Nightmare

Contents (cont.)

Part 4:

Mirage

Coffee

Nostalgia

Desire

My Dearest Love

The Road: Part One

The Road: Part Two

The Last Time

Just Scenes

In Autumn

To Evoke

Connect with the Author

FOREWORD

I put this collection together with the ultimate goal of finally getting some of my writing out there into the big bad world.

With all honesty, this is not a happy little book. I have struggled for over a decade with anxiety and depression, and all of what you read here stems from trying to cope with that. I hope though that if you relate to any of my writing, it helps you as well to process those feelings and begin to heal – as it has done for me.

Please make sure you read the trigger warning page before you proceed, and remember to seek support from family, friends, or your doctor if you, as well, struggle with a little bit of a void inside you.

And remember - Though the void seems endless and dark, starlight is often burning nearby, just waiting for you to see it.

- C. L. Adams

CONTENT WARNING – PLEASE READ BEFORE YOU PROCEED

As stated in the foreword, the works in this book may be triggering when read, so if you are affected by any of the topics below, please proceed with caution.

- Nightmares
- Self-harm
- Suicide ideation
- Abuse
- Panic attacks
- Depression
- Anxiety
- Medication

PART ONE

If I open myself up to write, and embrace my melancholy, I may excise it to some degree - For all to See.

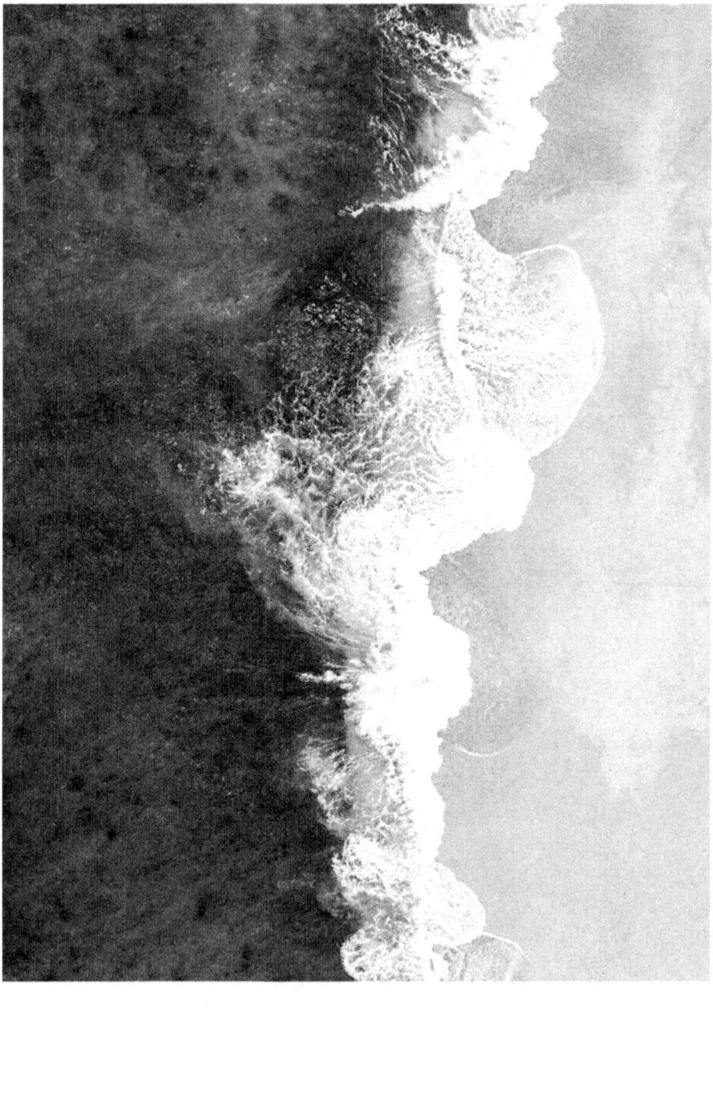

Oh, The Sea

How often I have written of you, but plenty more I have seen
you - in dreams, visions in daylight, frantic and vivid and
wonderful.

Stillness. Oh, you temptress,
Divine in the moonlight, I will never leave you,
As you have never left my thoughts for long.

But your rage - my goodness,
The things I have seen - how your power can move even the
ground beneath our feet -
The monuments I would build brick by brick in ode to you,
only for them to be washed away?

Thrilling delight, if only I could go with them.

-

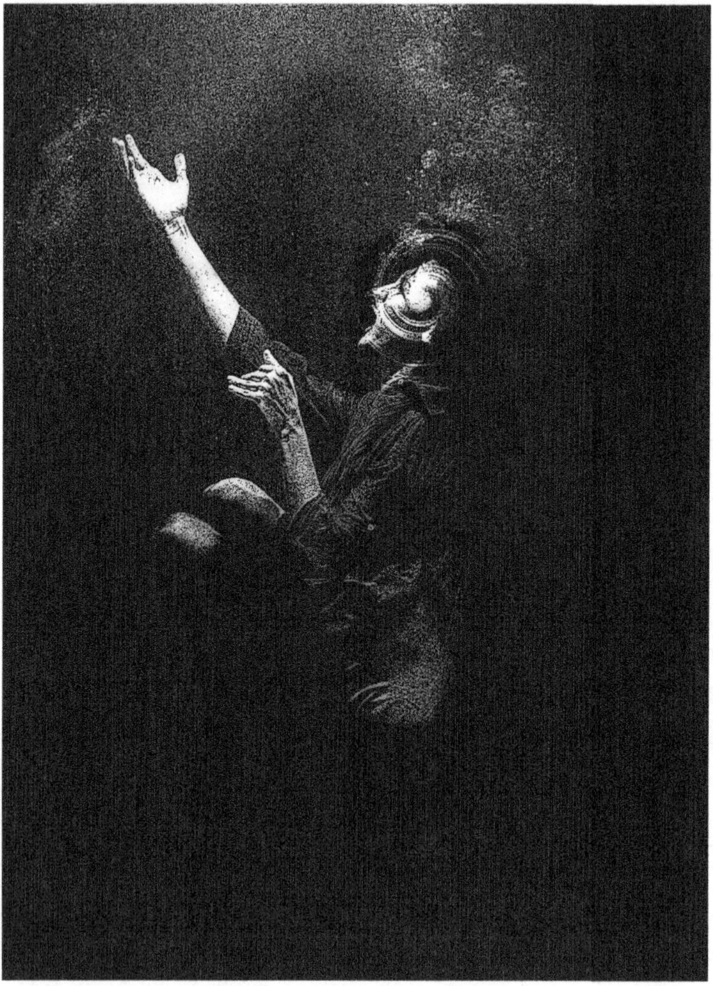

This too, I leave

I don't think I can adequately write or finish a story where
some element of you is missing.

Be it the pain you left in me,
Teasing smile or hint of the way I held you -

Yet when I write about you, that too
I can never quite get through without abandoning.

Succulent masochism.

-

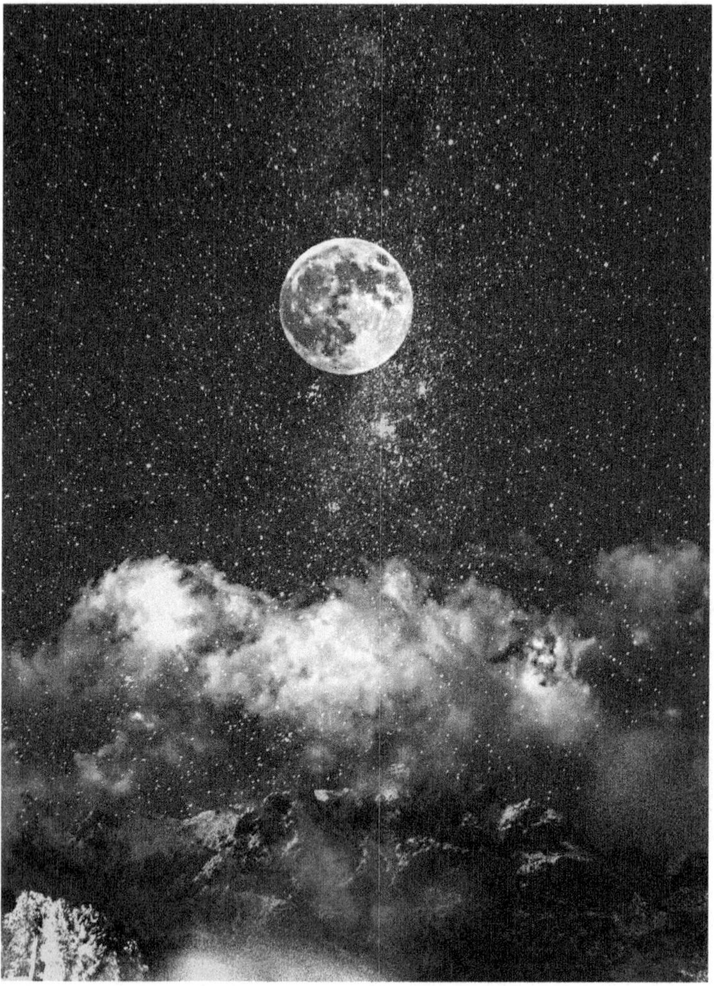

Stargazing

Frosted breath and only this
That I feel, squinting at a darkened sky to spot
Distant burning light, millennia old witnessed in this small way
Childish eyes, dreaming of that unattainable beauty above.

So oft, I return to those nights,
My camaraderie with the moon became more,
Now when I see Her,
I am comforted that it is not only I that remembers.

-

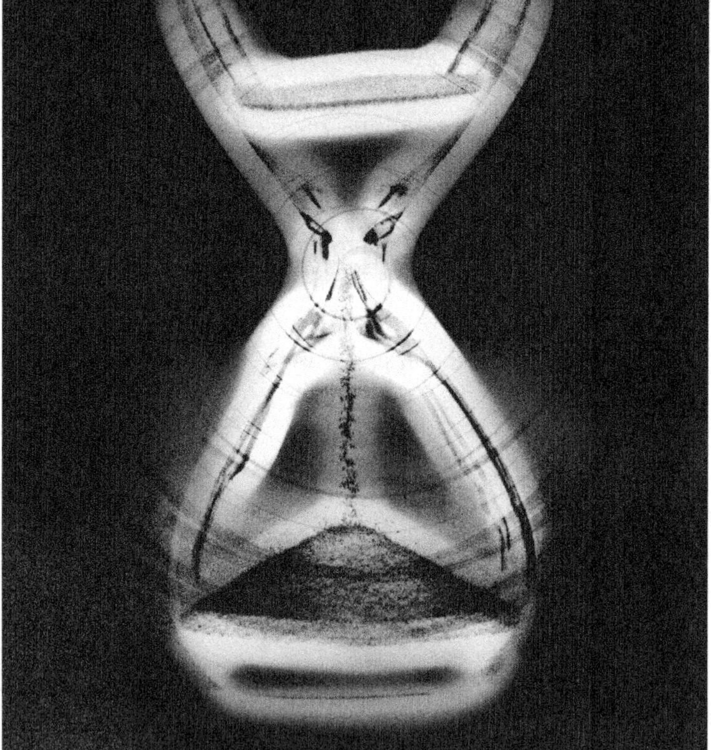

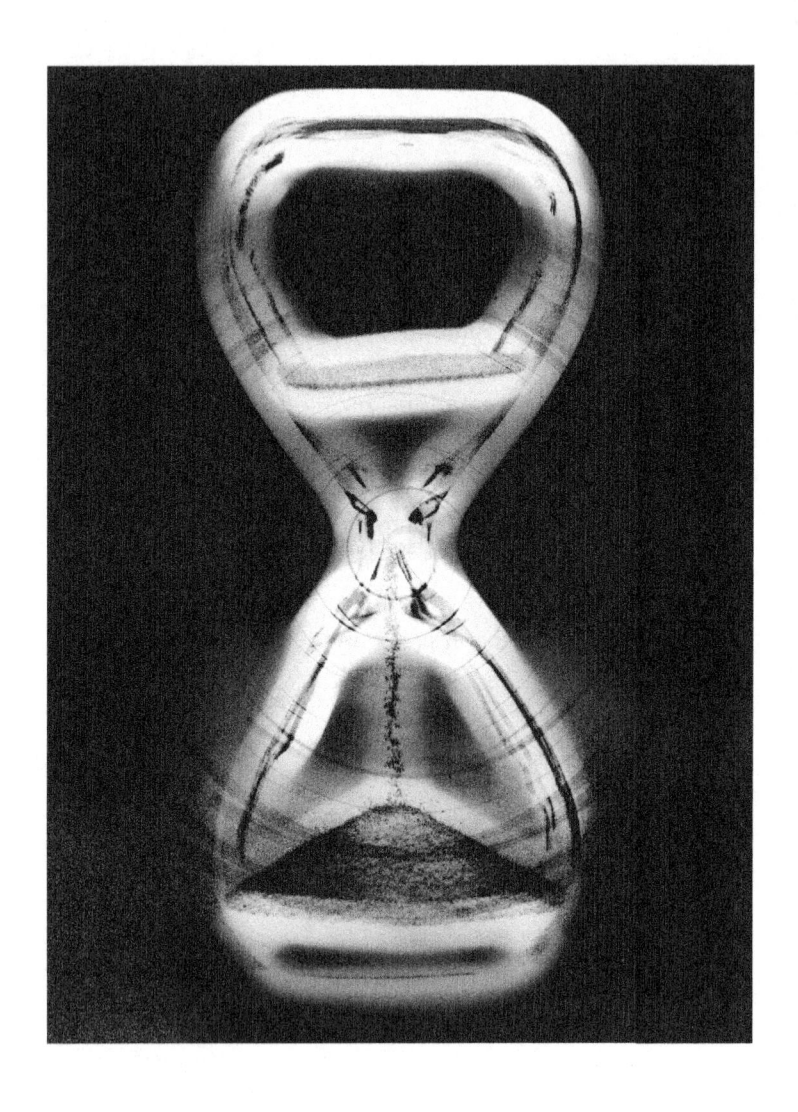

Static

So comforting to wrap yourself up in your decades old pain,
Too churlish - nay, too afraid to let it go because then: Who are you?

Answered already, defined by what happened then - both scared of repeating the past,
And more terrifying: What if you don't?

Well, ponder this premise:
Living in the past means your future has already been determined and lived.

-

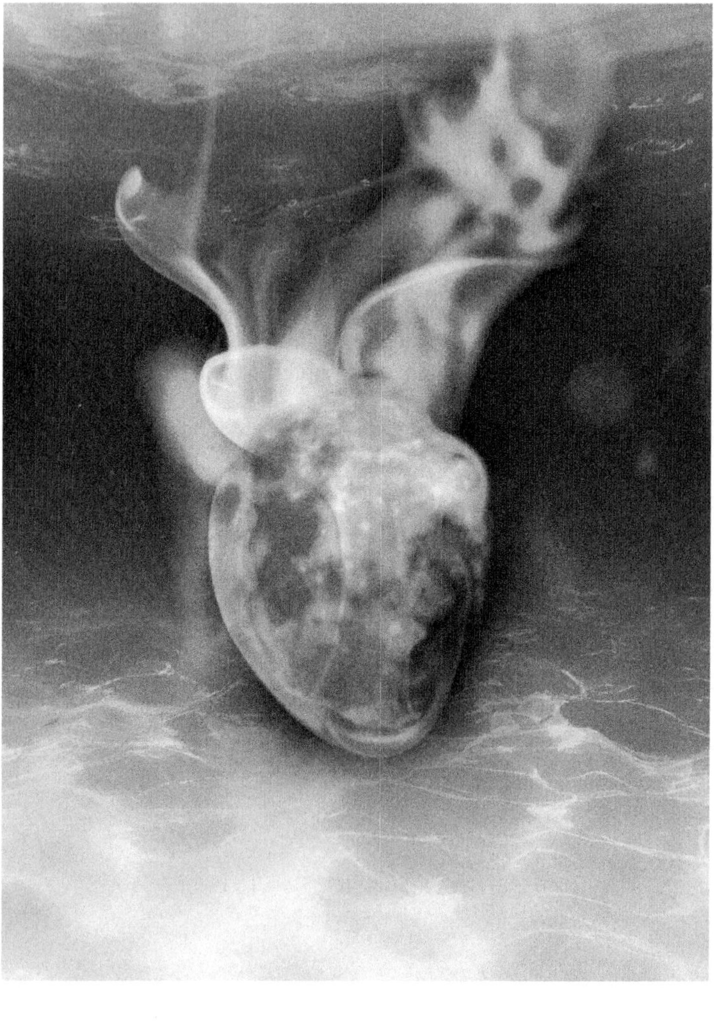

Filled With Void

My soul has already been claimed by the sea,
My heart by the moon,
My mind scattered with the stars.

I walk the Earth, stare into every river and stream I find,
Perhaps wondering if the key to drowning the monster inside me is in those depths,
Perhaps imagining wrongly that I'd be caressed by the waves instead of frozen and crushed by a power I was too naive to believe in.

Bleeding heart, of course,
Any injury merely strikes an emptied chest and gouges the cavity deeper.

I used to have passion,
learning was a thrill and a pleasure,
I would reach those stars and follow in their footsteps only too literally -
Now I burn.

-

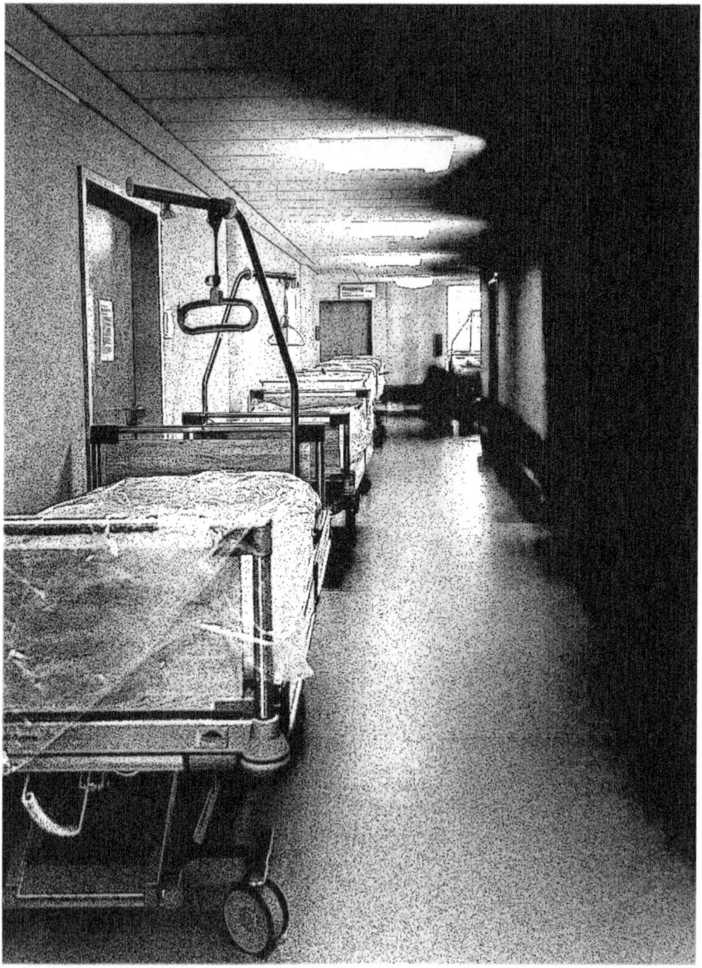

Exhausted

Truly, I thought once I was finding catharsis,
When visions of blood came to me,
The natural conclusion was to make it real, to purge those thoughts.

All I got were scars.

Nightmares too,
Clingy, those visions never really left,
I clench my jaw when they creep up on me,
ride out the wave.

Why am I learning to swim in the deep end, still?

-

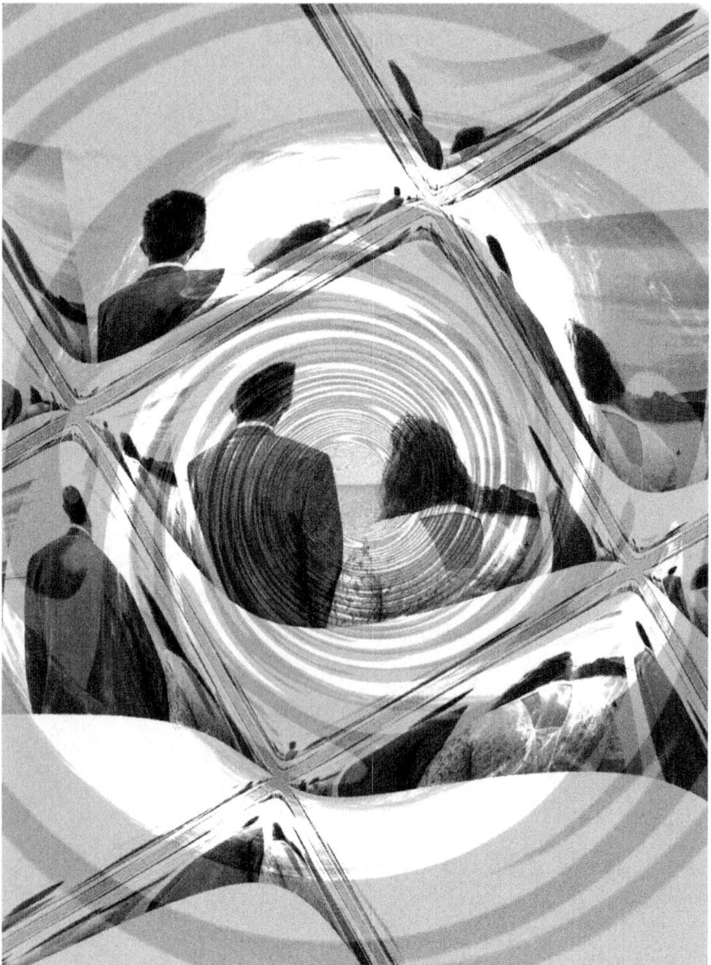

Oasis

Maybe I need to up my dose,
My lungs heavy as lead pin me to this sofa.

If my pain is usually kept in a neat little box in my chest,
The lock has corroded.

I dare not give up,
Even as fog clouds my thoughts,
I feel the sofa soft and terrible against my skin as the buzzing silence tears at me.

Too much, I throw myself to the floor and find Him - he wraps me in arms that do not hurt like so much scratchy fabric. He murmurs, and his voice does not tear at me.

-

PART TWO

Less purposefully, and without intention to let my heart see the light of day, this mania driven rambling now exposed - to then cut out the rot growing in that dark void.

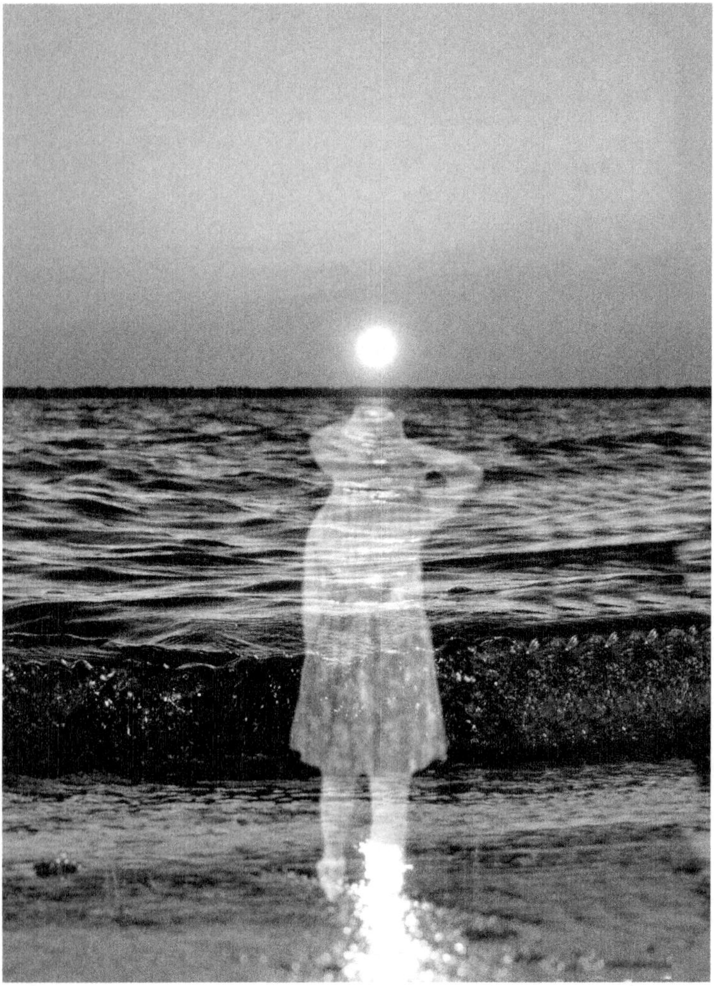

15.06.14

I was once a little girl,
In the big wide world,
And all the time, I felt afraid.

I loved and lost,
As little girls do,
When mistakes and misjudgments are made.

But I was once a little girl,
Desperate to feel and he…
He made me feel alive.

-

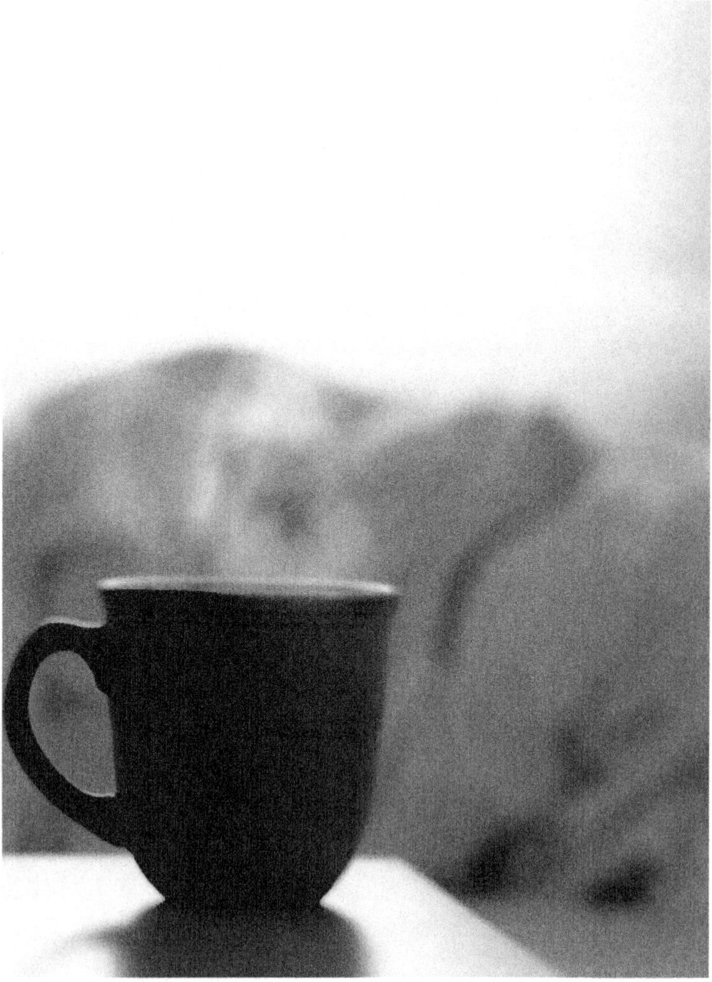

01.11.14

That feeling where things seem to lull,
Where the whole world must be busy and frantic with movement,
But alone -
Nothing seems to move at all.

Times slips by,
It doesn't matter that much,
Because nothing else seems to exist,
Nothing at all.

The dull, boring ache of a lonely afternoon,
Drifting through notes,
Drifting through thoughts, and feelings,
Waiting for forever for some sort of movement.

Maybe if something happened,
My Saturday wouldn't seem so drab,
So grey,
I'm still waiting for colours to bloom out of nothing.

-

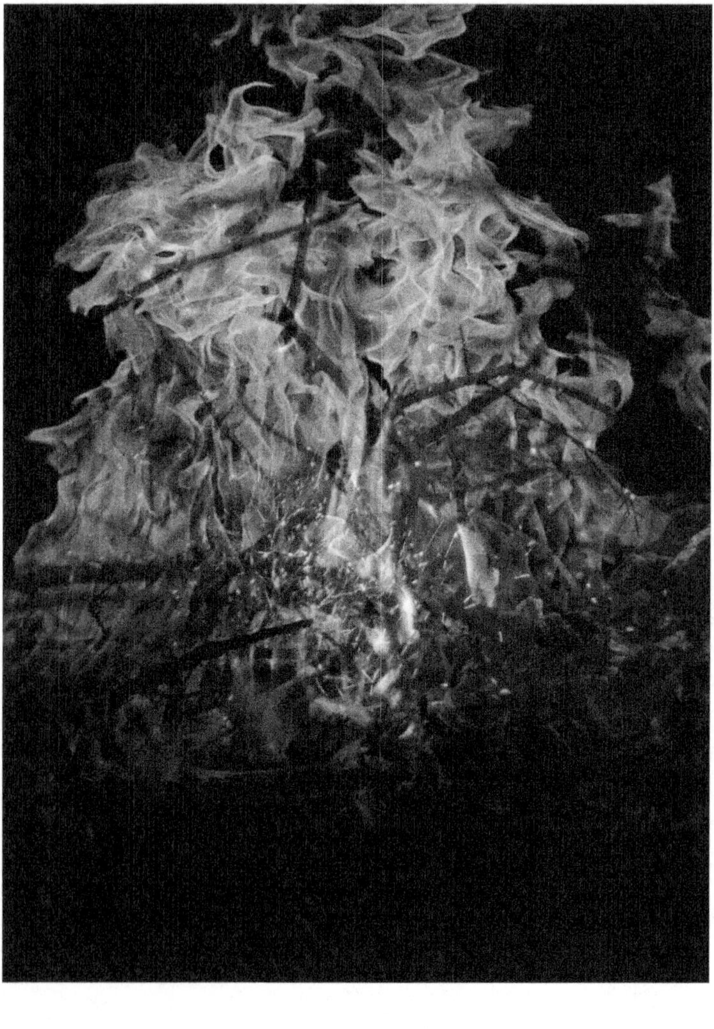

10.11.14

Forcing my hand into my mouth,
Biting down on my tongue,
Holding back the screams.

Deep disappointment tears across my heart,
And I remember everything.

It only takes one word.

-

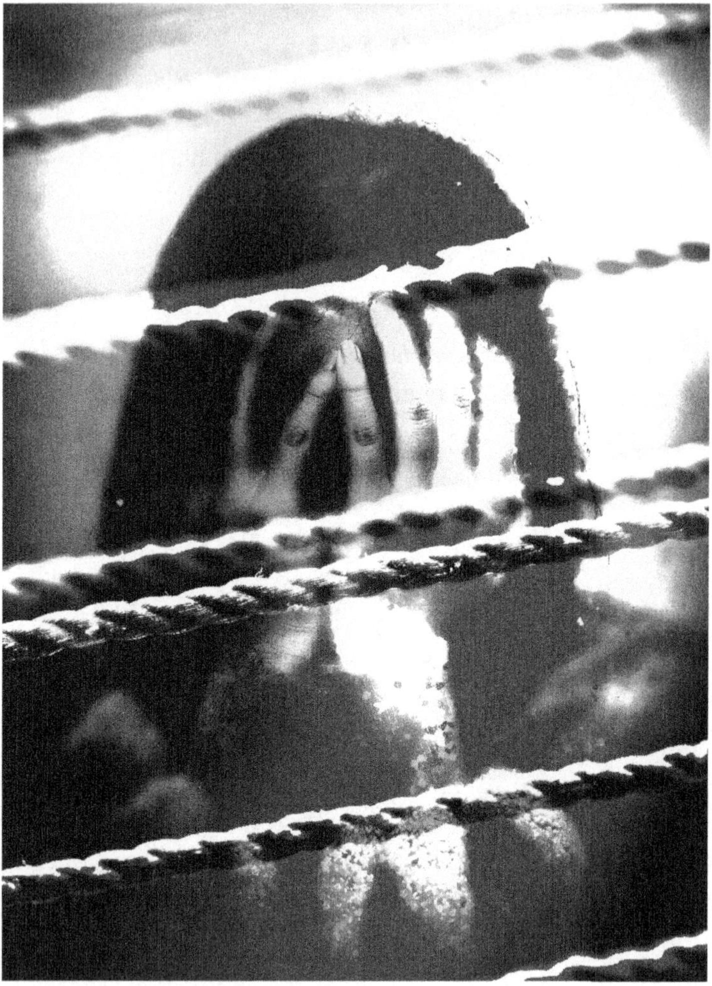

22.03.15

The cruel edge of a blade beckons my chest,
While ropes seduce me into being bound so tightly that my breath escapes,
My fingers and toes becoming blue,
My lips betraying death with their slight exhale.

This that plagues,
And ultimately drains me,
Until the only energy left drives me numbly to a sinister goal,
I feel that the fight has just begun.

At the end,
Will it be clear if I have won?

-

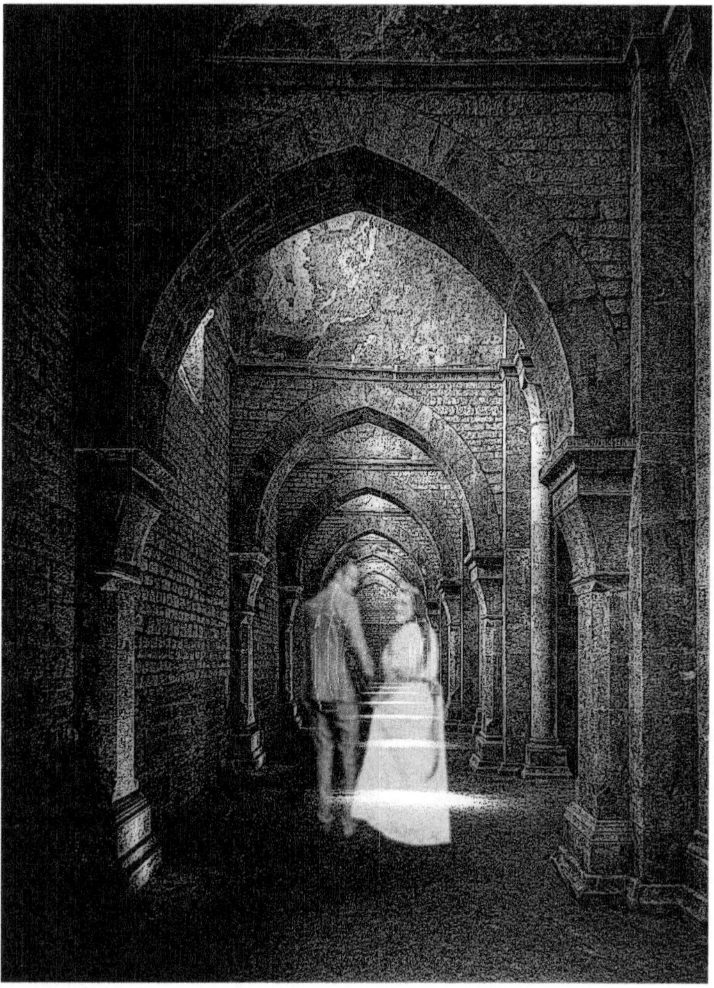

20.06.15

Like a ghost,
I wandered the house,
No one else home.

I sought out the breath of life,
It was disappointing, the search,
My gasping lungs found no such breath to drive the death out of my body.

Instead,
I found a pen, I wrote,
And sung until I could no more.

Then He returned, home at last,
I breathed him in,
And found my lungs were delighted.

He is life itself,
And a ghost I am:
No more.

-

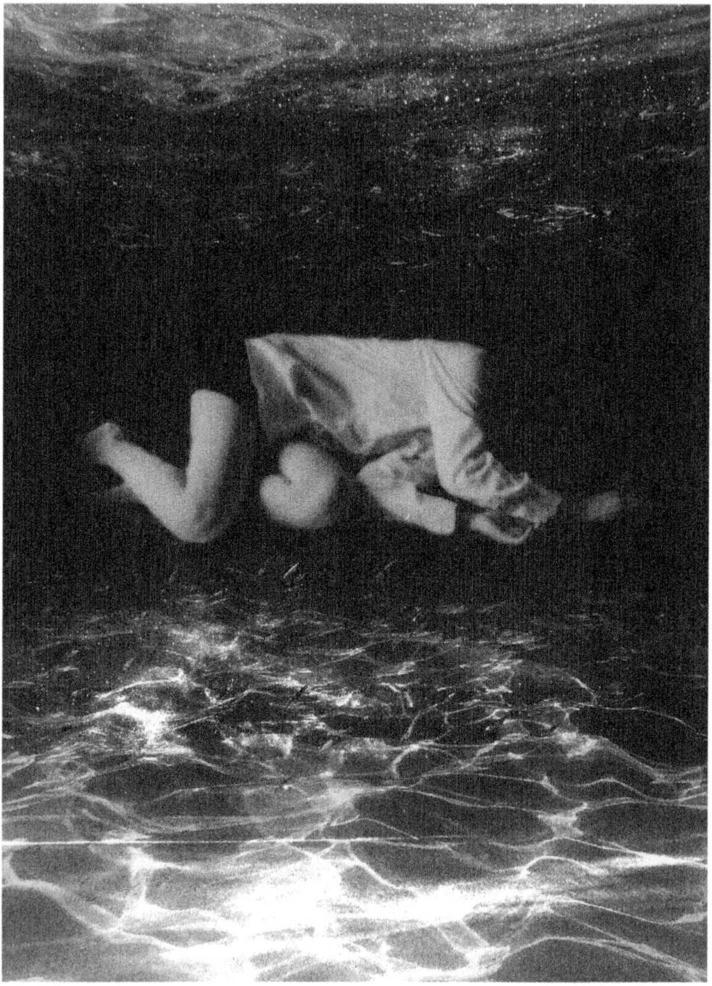

23.03.16

I was freezing in my self-imposed shell,
When a star burned me until I was lukewarm,
Now unsure if I am cold again or due a fever,
I fall from the clouds I'd hidden in,
And drown in lakes and waterfalls of starlight,
Forever seeking a comet to find refuge in,
Orbiting the lonely sun I've always admired,
Wondering if it would ever burn me too,
Or maybe forge me anew from dust.

I sleep, freezing in my hesitant wait,
Until the fierceness of the Sun's death will rage over us all,
And in fire I will, perhaps, become a star too.

-

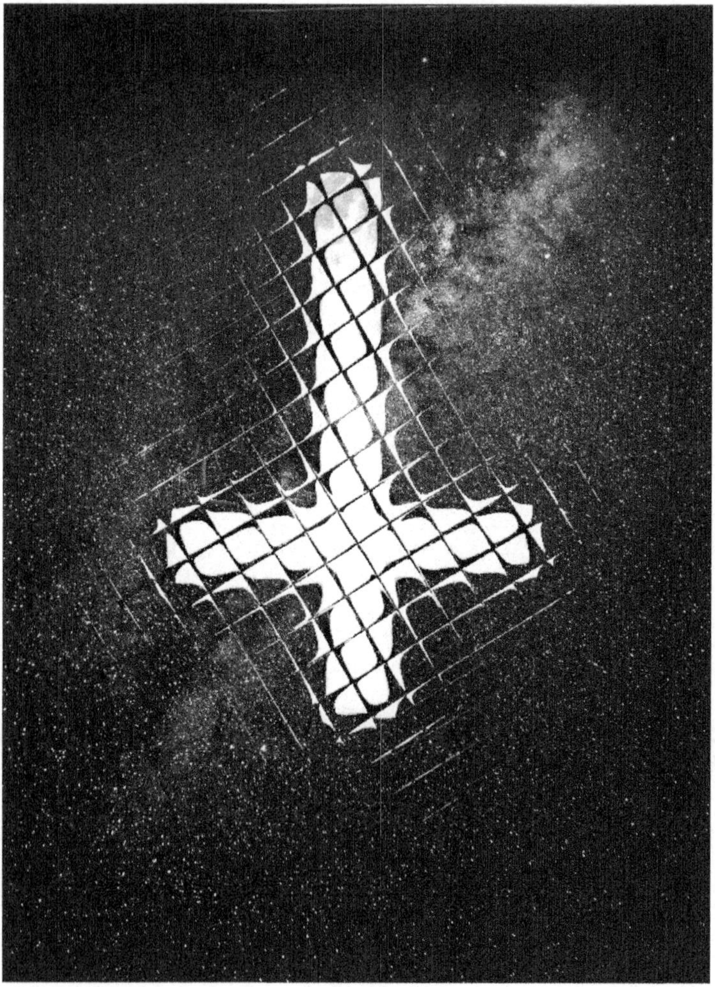

10.03.17

What is it about the deplorable that brings such delight to me?
And in such delight, why do they find me to be such a wicked sight?

Day becomes night, and I
Alone with the stars,
Take a breath,
And exhale my yesterdays, for tonight::

I am alive.

-

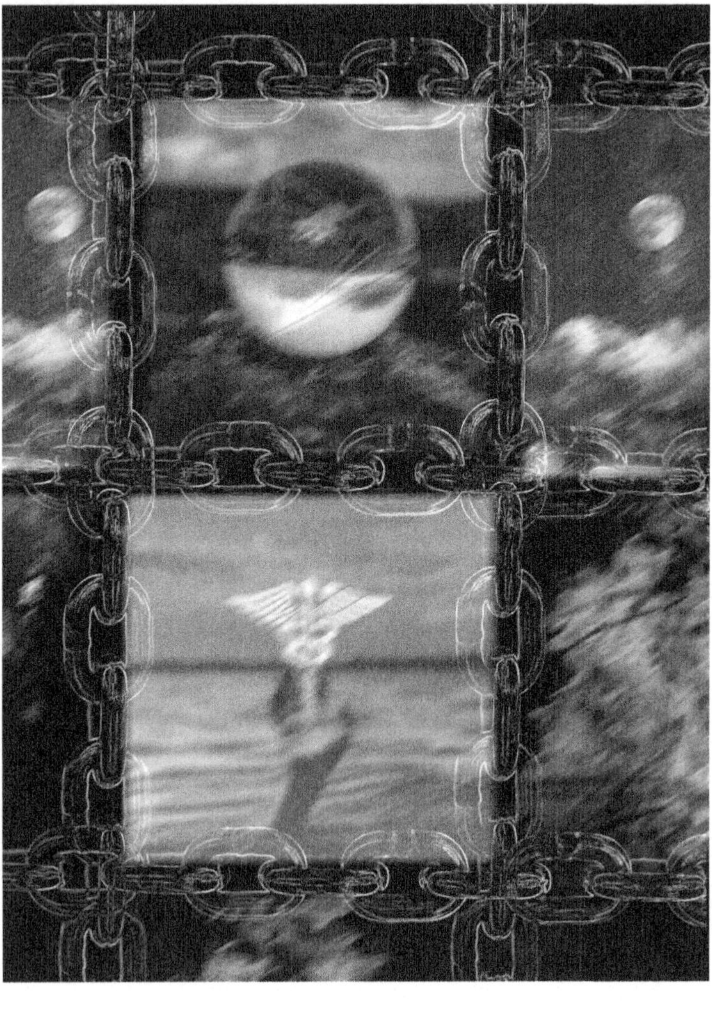

27.06.18

I still carry you with me,
A chain of fire around my neck,
The fist curled around my lungs,
The traitor tear escaping my eye as I find my pleasure,
And my mind skips to you almost immediately.

You did tell me you wanted me to remember you,
The things we did together,
And though I would sooner scream than say it,
I do.

-

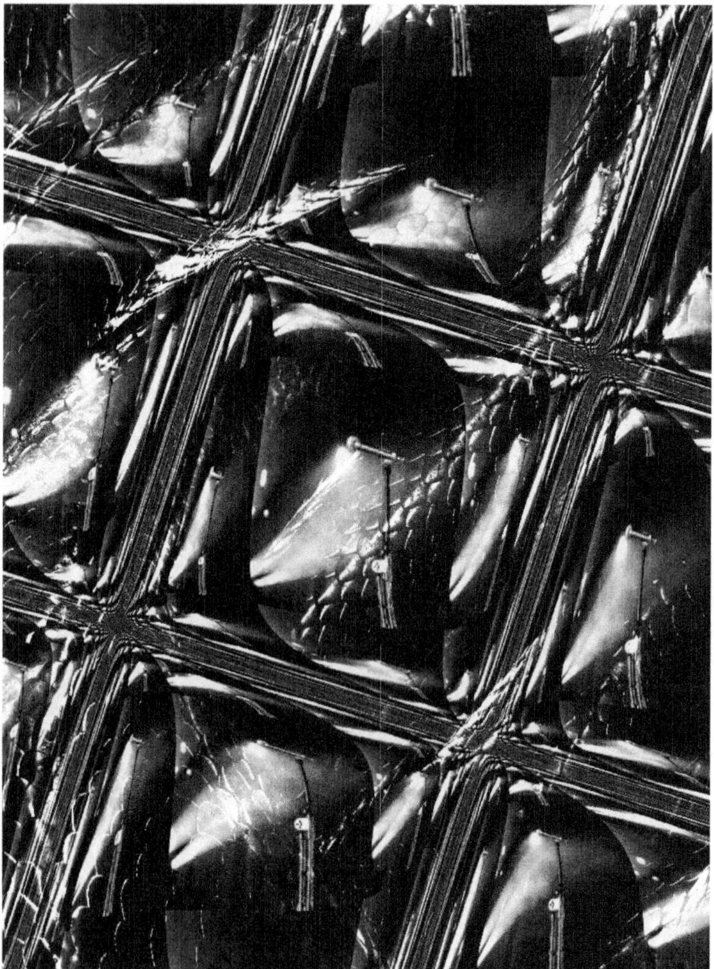

10.01.19

Singing is not quite screaming,
But it is the closest I can get,
Give to me the heart-wrenching cries of passionate souls,
Let me hear their pain,
So I can add my voice to their chorus and carry their story with me always.

When is a song not a song?

-

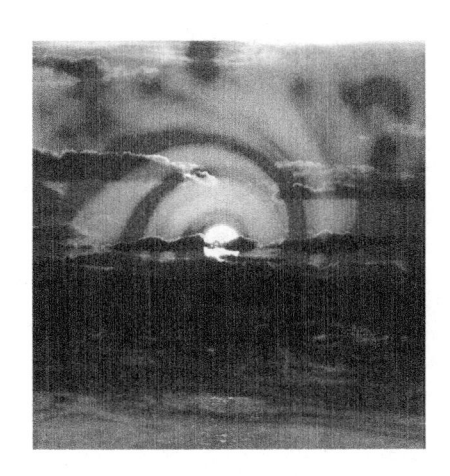

PART THREE

And so, cast out by so much ire - I simmer down. Only to find the sun setting again. What madness is this, that it should fail to relent after such measures?

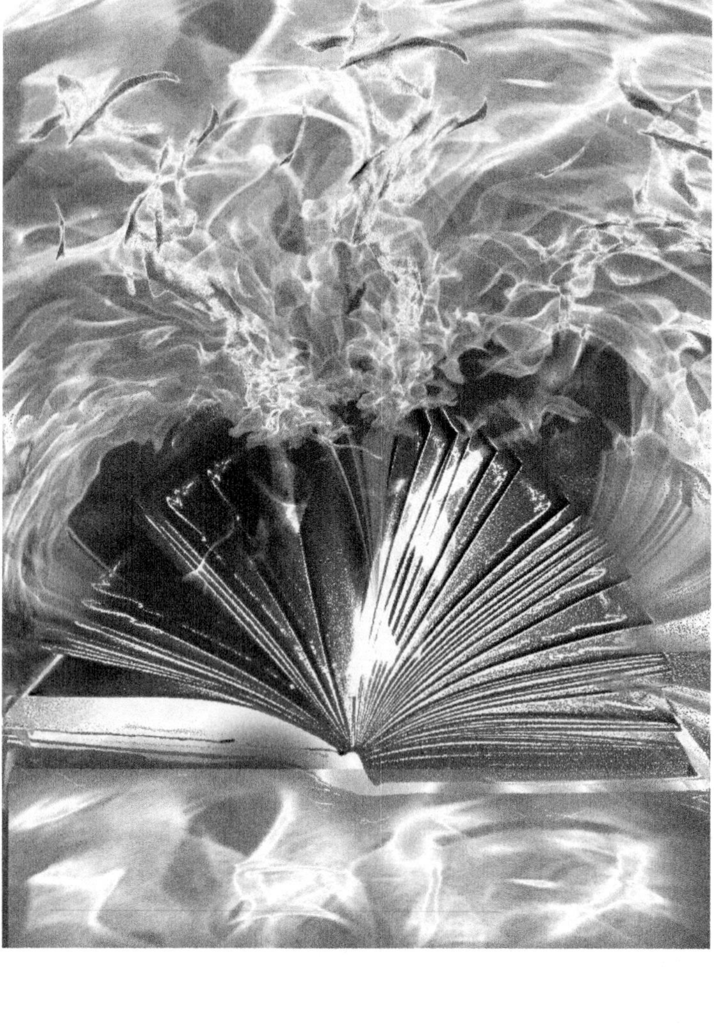

Ember

Of the thousand letters I wrote in Ode to you,

Not a single one survived the flames of morning,

But this.

-

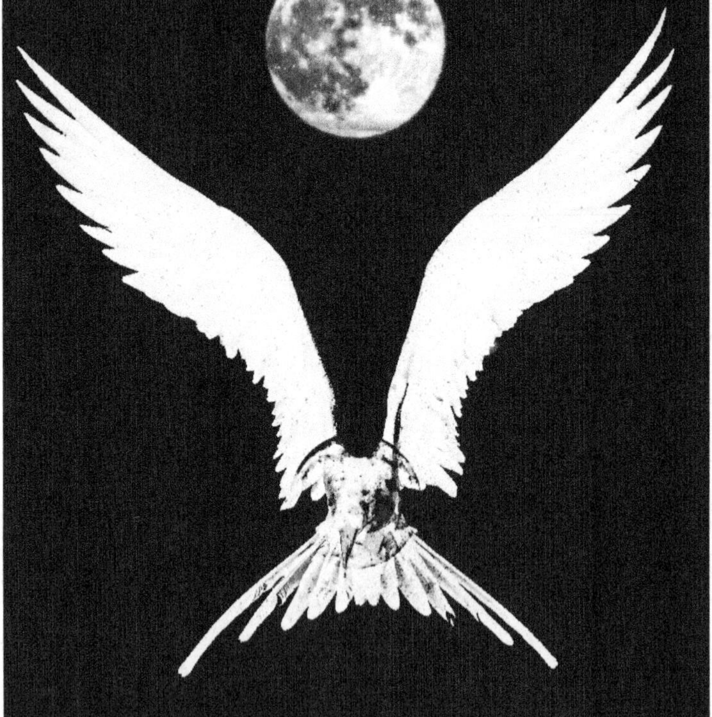

Vengeance

Look upon me and mourn.

Hear my voice in delight.

At night,

It will tear your dreams apart.

-

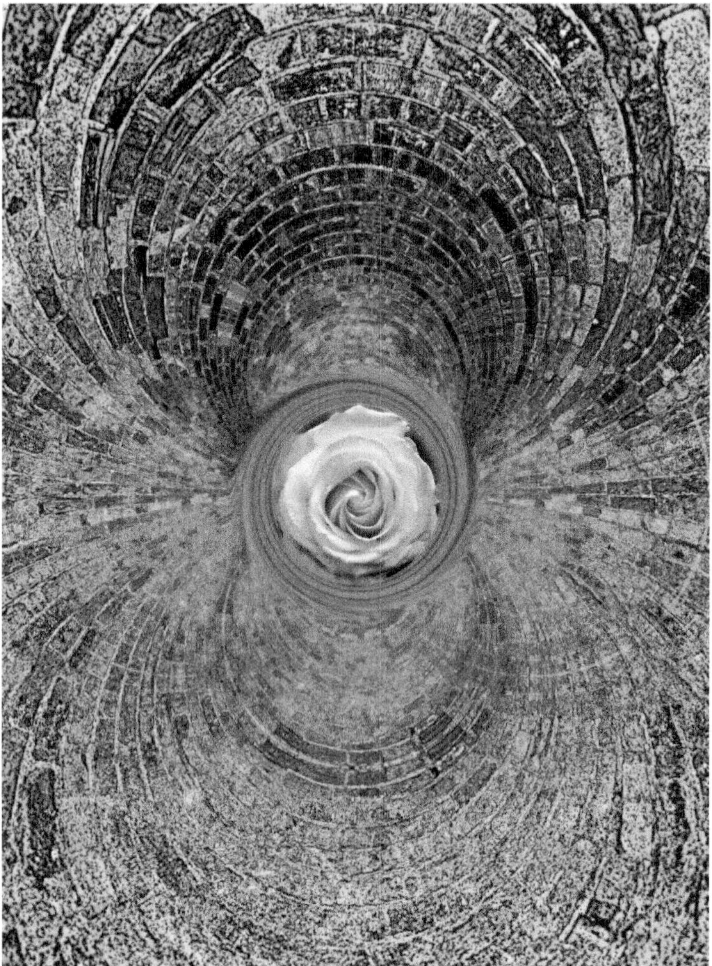

Mortar

That love feels so long ago,

My life has happened in such vast quantities since then that

You feel like part of the foundations

I have built myself on.

-

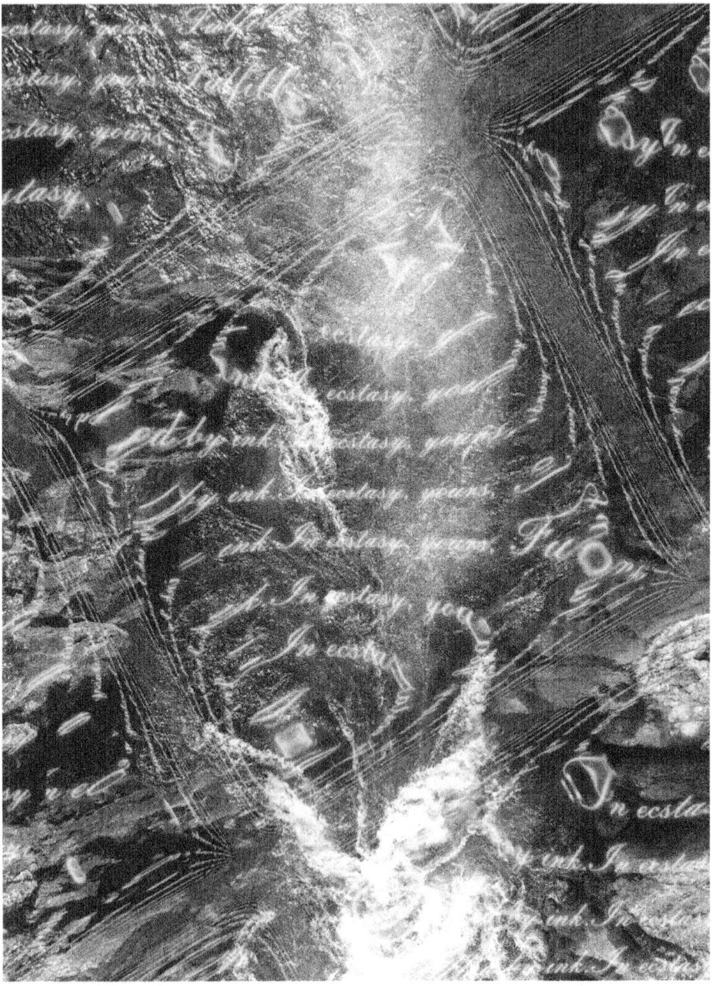
ink. In ecstasy, yours.

Desiderium

A talented enough hand need never touch me,

Your written words caress my candlelight core,

A heady drug, my skin alight,

Eyes greedy,

I am dizzy with it,

And God, I can't stop myself from tending the fire.

In ecstasy, yours,

Fulfilled by ink.

-

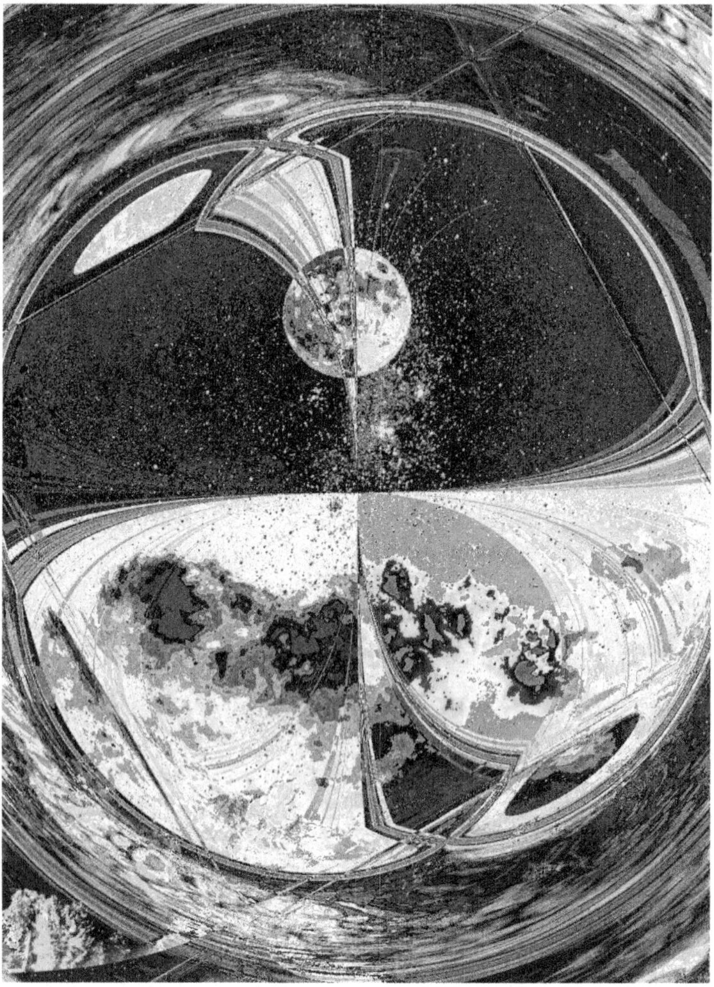

Fractured

I want to write about you, and even though I feel furiously the words biting to get out, there's just so much to say that it gets hard to write much at all.

~

Look upon me and mourn.
Hear my voice and delight:
It will tear your dreams apart.

~

You're bottled up inside me,
Some frenzied part of my brain holds on, clings to every word as gospel.

~

Time does not bend away from you,
still.

~

I damn you still for having crossed my path,
Yet dread the thought of never knowing you again.

-

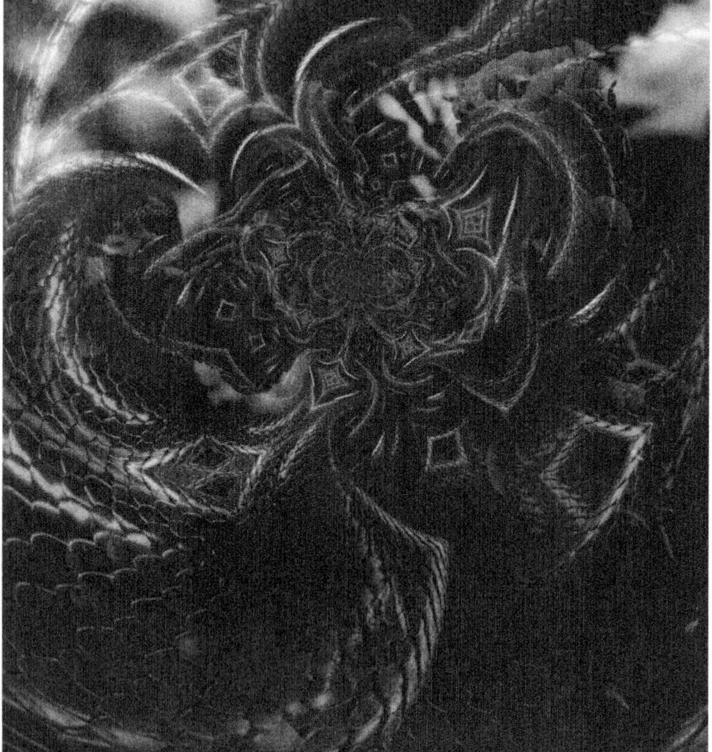

Nightmare

If I keep leaving parts of myself in the dream world,

Will I disappear?

I awaken with the sense that I could have stayed gone.

-

PART FOUR

The sun has set and now the moon may rise, soothing my burning soul until my fever calms. Now, to stand at the window and gaze upward through city lights to where my heart lives. Might I rest with ease at last?

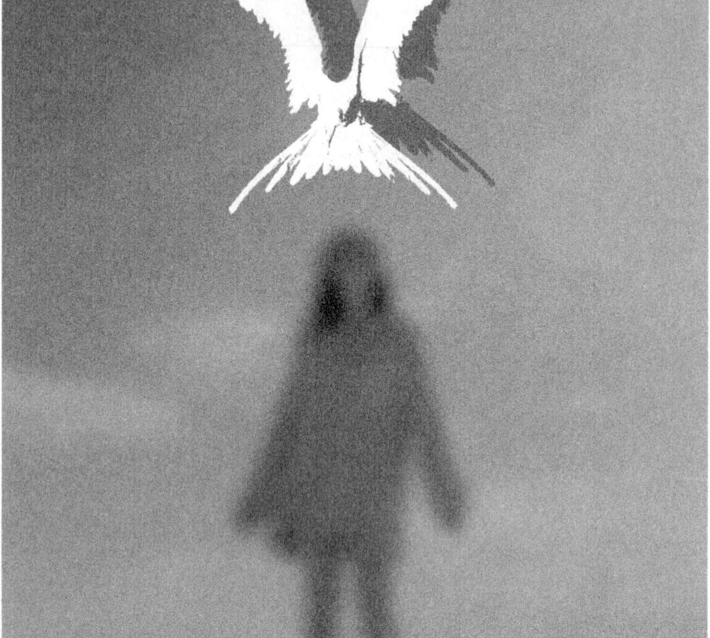

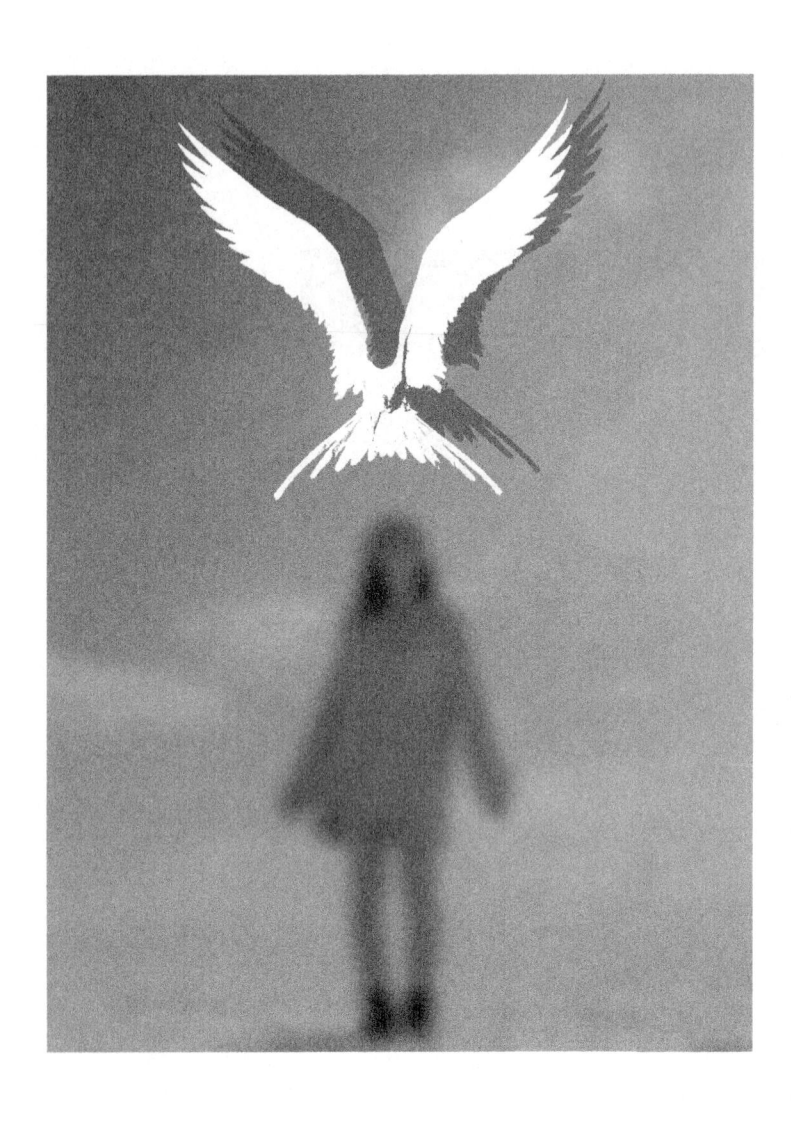

Mirage

Memories of memories,
Whispers of touch,
I only know how I
Craved you, so much.

Yet - I may be forgetting how it felt to be yours.

It has burned into me
For a decade,
Or more
And decades to come.

I'll be chasing ghosts of your voice,
Your blessed face,
Your bitter promises,
Every moment I sink into contemplation.

Inevitably bidden by thought: that ideal, hazy figure,
So blinded.
My mirage
And my Heart.

-

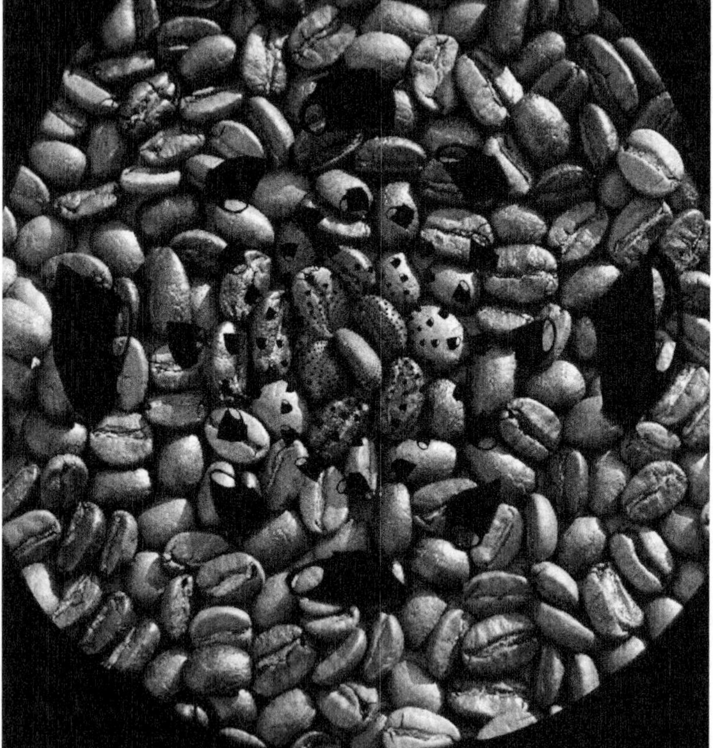

Coffee

I've lost count of the times
Coffee has painted
My lips
With pain

That
Brief
Blip
A brush of sensation

Hearing your name
Seeing your face
Is much like that

I once filled with contentment
And warmth and I felt like myself with you
Until I felt like I didn't know you
And so I lost myself too

And no amount of sugar is shifting
The bitter
Vile
Aftertaste from my tongue

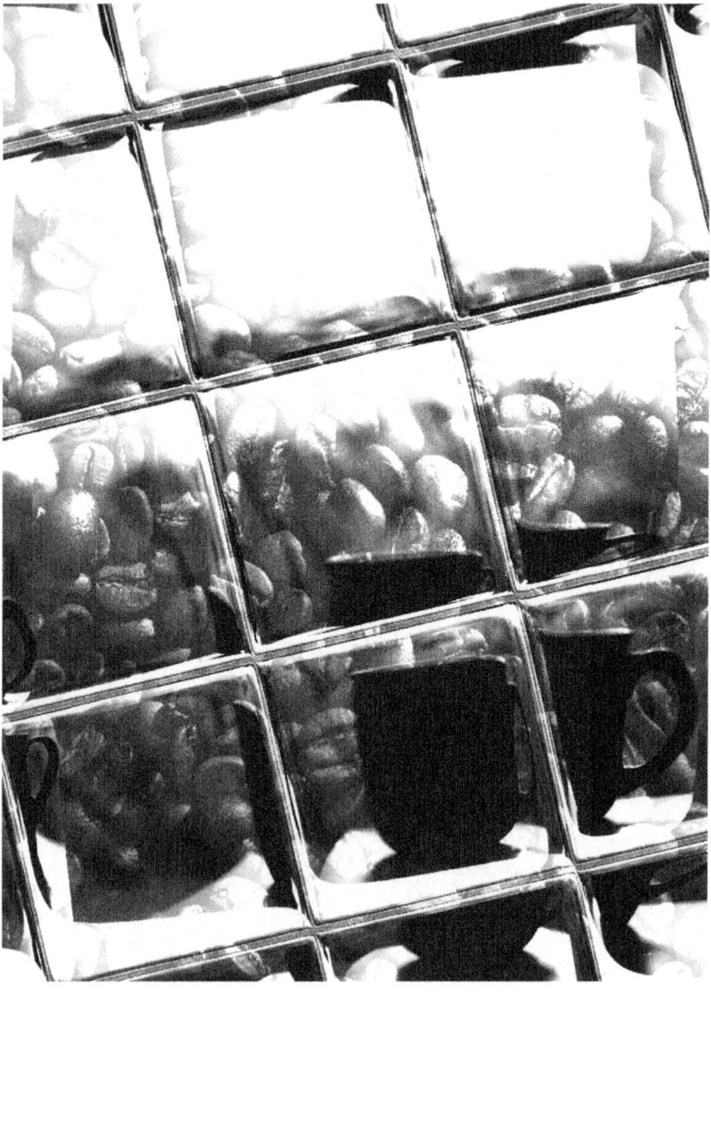

I am drowning in it
Recoiling from the memories
They burn as a kettle poured over my chest

And the way you once loved me
Now feels like choking on those grains so dry
I stuff myself with them until my throat bleeds and pretend it's normal to have coffee this way

But it's not
And you've ruined me.

-

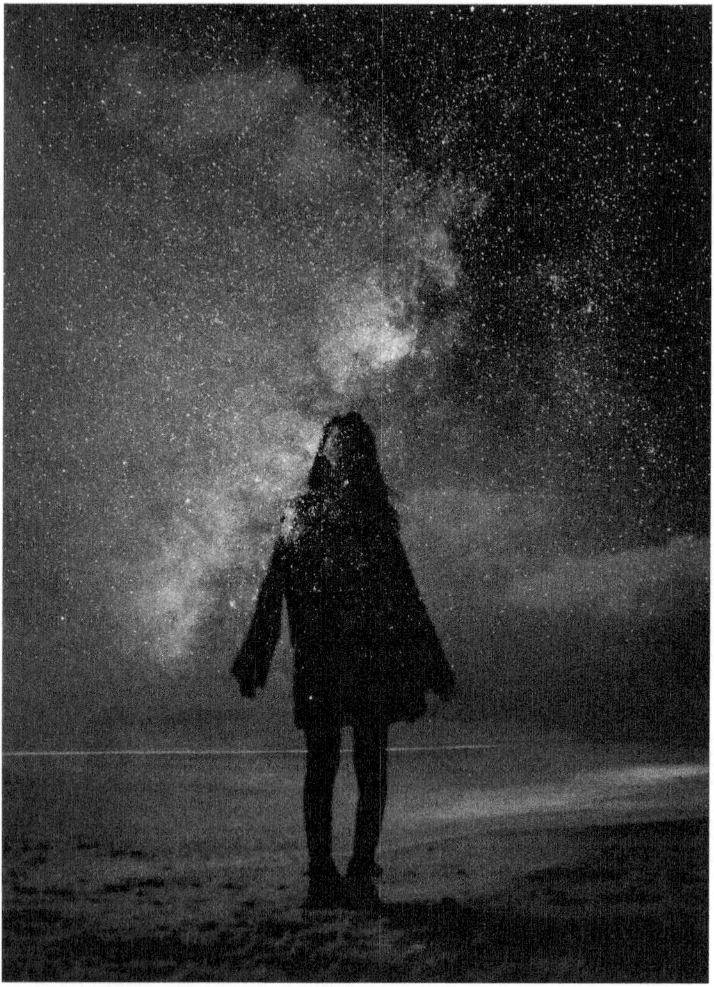

Nostalgia

So, when the evening came,
Despite the warmth of my lover's arms,
The comfort of home and the joys that the future would bring,
I spared a moment for yearning, for melancholy,
Because when I looked to the sky and thought hard,
Of beloved stars and all that I had yet to learn that I loved:

I missed simply standing in the cool night air at 2am,
Hoping to see a star flash for a second into my vision,
Drinking hot cocoa while bundled up in mother's old coat,
Running around the garden to see every angle of those constellations,
The simple joy a clear night sky could bring.

I sighed and the memories fell back into dust,
And I climbed into bed,
Safe and warm at 11pm,
While a piece of my heart dreamt on.

-

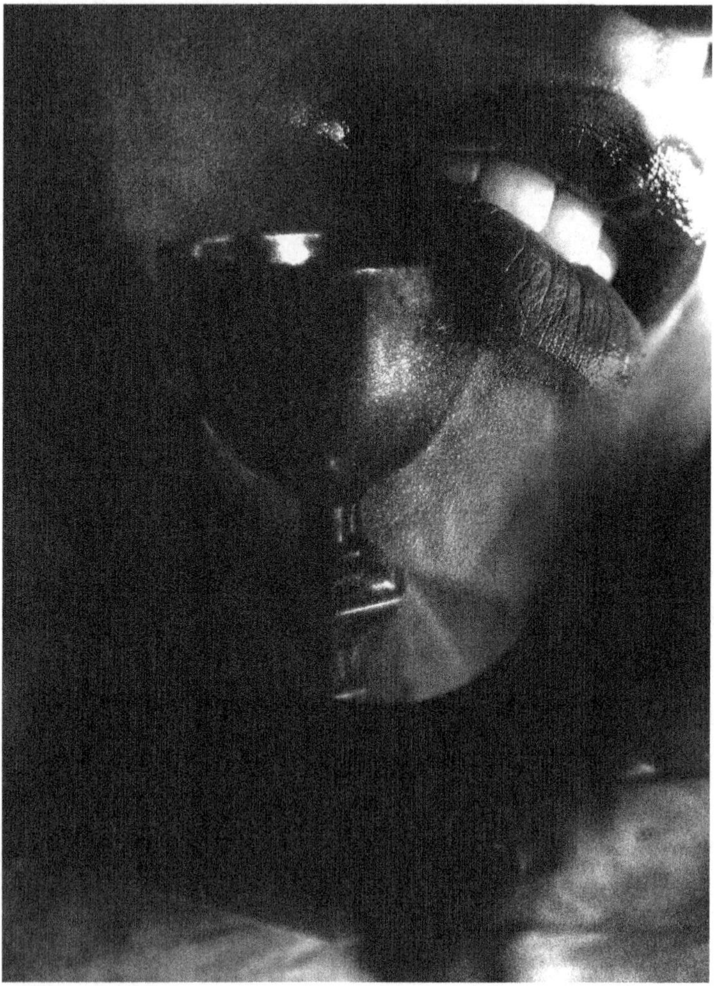

Desire

A thousand cups of wine could not slake his thirst,
But she had a beautiful mind,
And before he knew it -
A droplet fallen from her rosy lips had him on his knees,
He could bear no more.

So, thirst quenched yet soul in agony, he followed where she went
Until, one day, her face was marred by tears:
He drowned, and passed in a singular ecstasy.

-

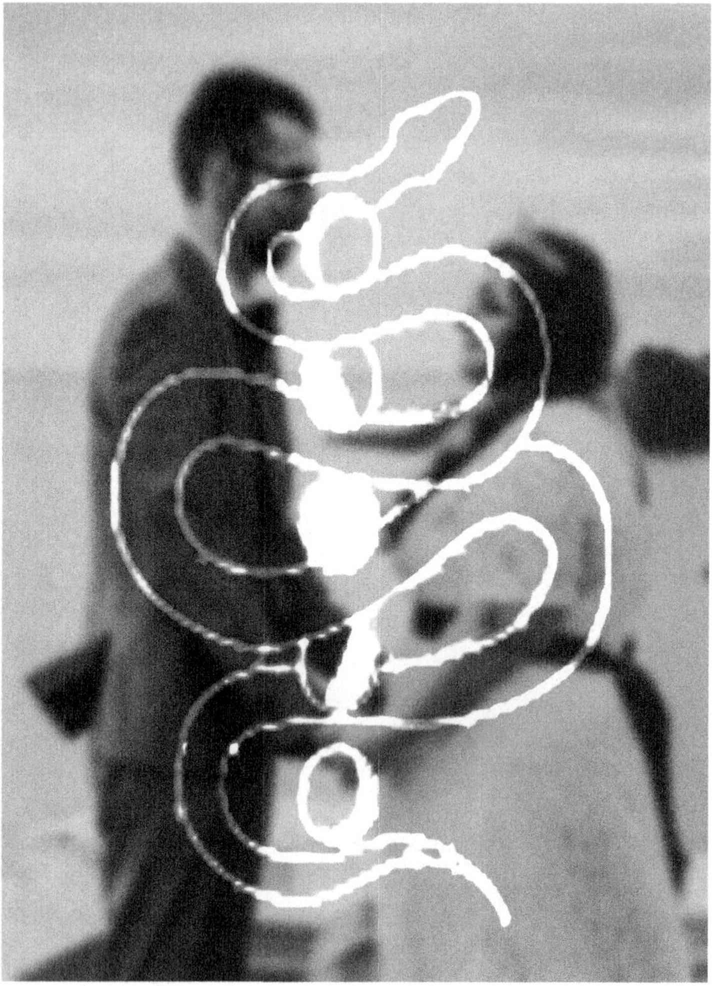

My Dearest Love

Of all that I have loved dearly in this world,
The stars have often been my most cherished,
I have looked to them many a night and each time felt wonder and belonging,
Our place in the cosmos is tiny, but nonetheless: Ours.

Imagine my surprise when I saw your face for the first time,
I felt that wonder,
Imagine, as you held me,
I felt intense belonging, a sense of rightness and of home.

After that,
It didn't take me long to realise that I love you more dearly than the stars.
You are more than even the idols and gods we humans seek in times of despair.

I have whispered your name reverently in darkness,
More than a prayer,
My faith in you goes beyond that of prayer.

I have kissed you and felt such love that it brings me to tears to think of it now.

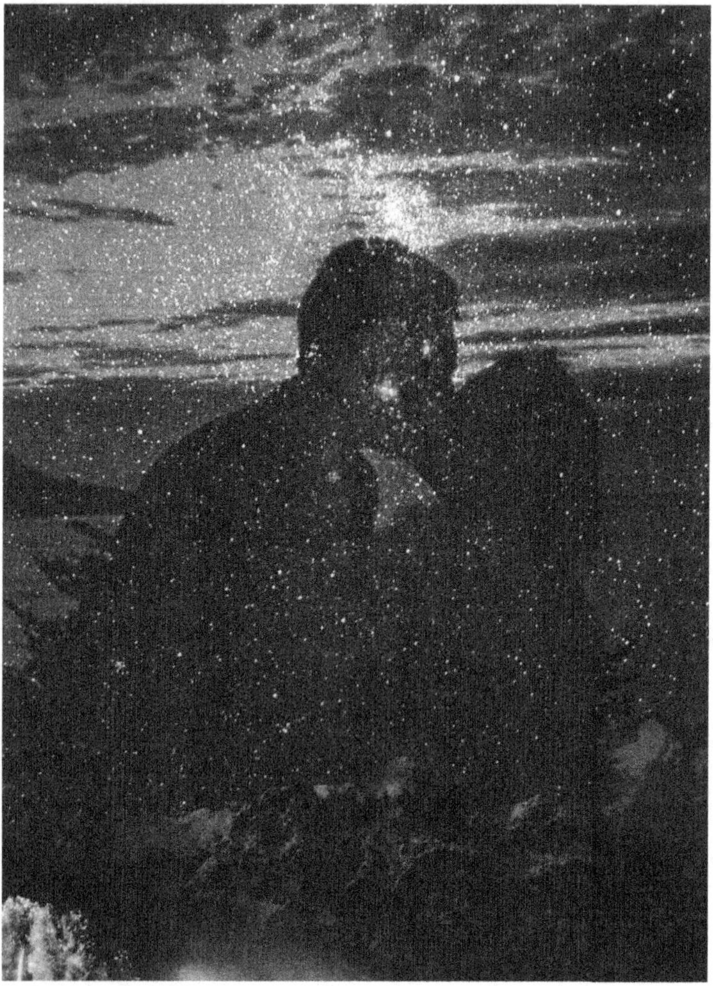

Yet,
You wonder why I worship you,
Why I want to be as close to you as I can be?

You are more than divinity,
More than the stardust in our veins,
And to kiss you a thousand times would never be enough.

My love,
Let me hold you,
Please you,
Bring you happiness and bliss -
Because if I had to see you frown for even a moment,
My heart might stop.

My precious one,
I hope you can understand how much I love you,
How much I need you to show me that in this vast cosmos:
I am not alone in the intensity of my feelings.

Let me lose myself in you,
It is my most elaborate form of addiction,
And most expressive form of love that I know how to give you.

-

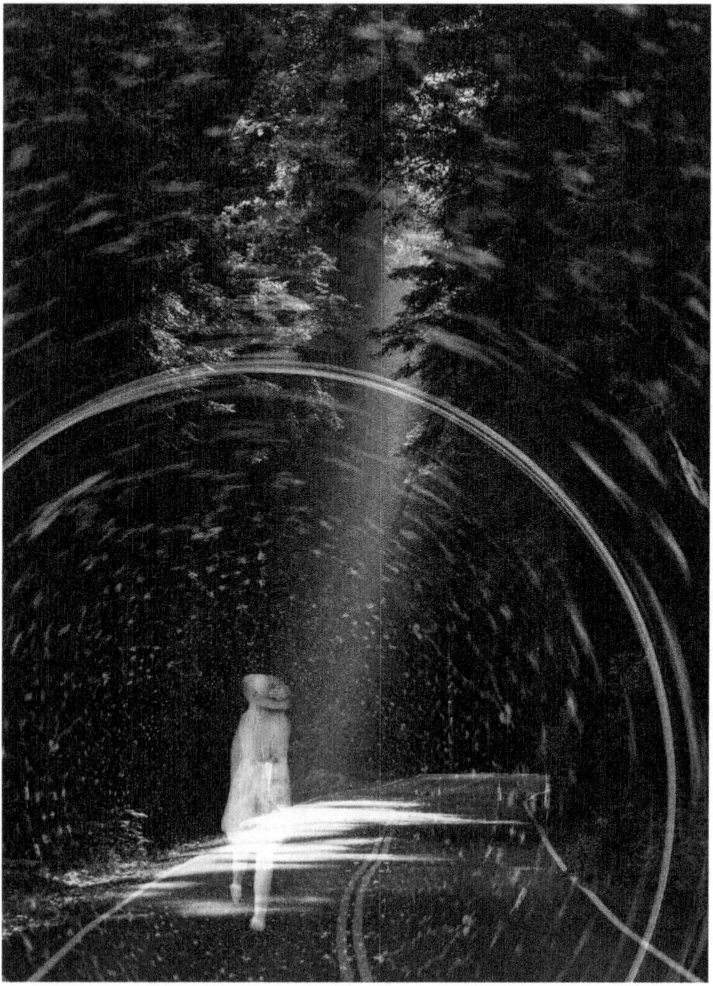

The Road: Part One

One road, a lonely road,
Full of people who strive,
It's a path I could take, but I hesitate,
There are other roads too.

Pushed and commanded towards the lonely road,
I open my eyes and finally see:
There's suddenly another way,
A new study, a different road.

But after forcing myself a few years along the loneliest road,
Can I divert from my route?
What if the light I see is a cruel, harsh one?
But... What if this road is a better one?

Choosing my road never felt like a choice before,
But a hand extends and clasps mine tight,
The choice is mine alone,
I have chosen.

-

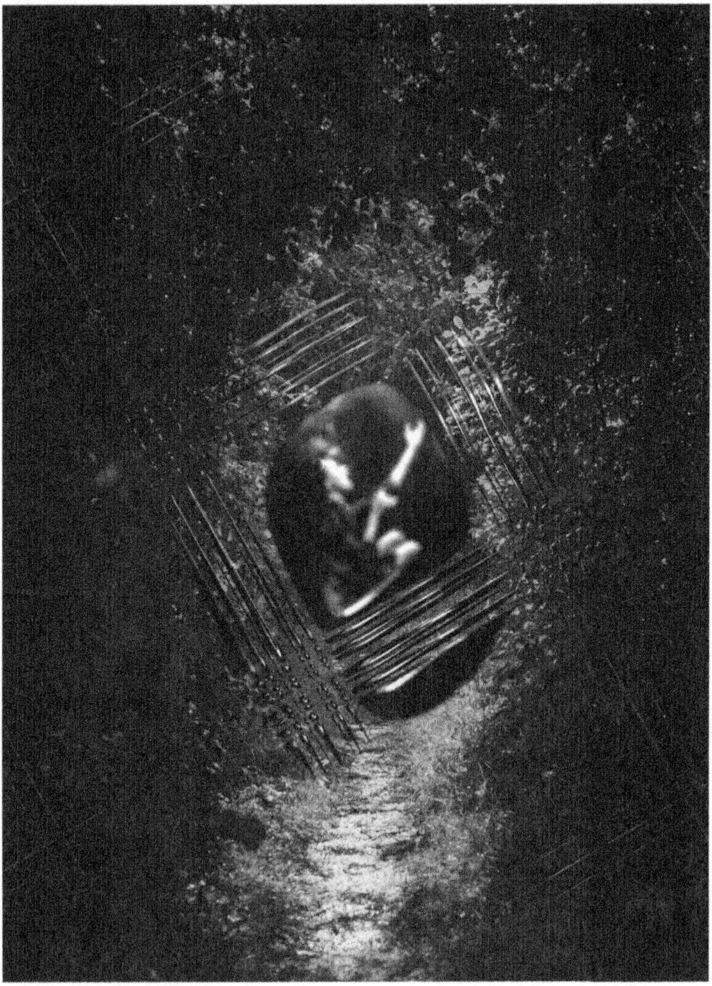

The Road: Part Two

Weary as ever I wander along a worn out road,
Hands buried deep in my pockets,
Hair covering my face as I stare at the ground,
And I wonder: Why now?

Trembling lips curl in a mocking smile,
Like yours,
Only mine are coated with scars and dried blood,
All of the biting was for nought in the end.

Dust blows without regret to my eyes,
Unwilling tears spring forth,
A surprise!
I had thought to be dried of my tears.

Unprotected knees meet the hard concrete,
More blood spilt onto the distanced soil,
My fists are clenched as your face appears in my mind,
Sickness prevails as your words resound in my head.

Alone I kneel,
But I feel your eyes on me,
I feel your phantom nails scrape along my throat,
Tilting my chin upwards so that you might see my filthy, tear-stained face.

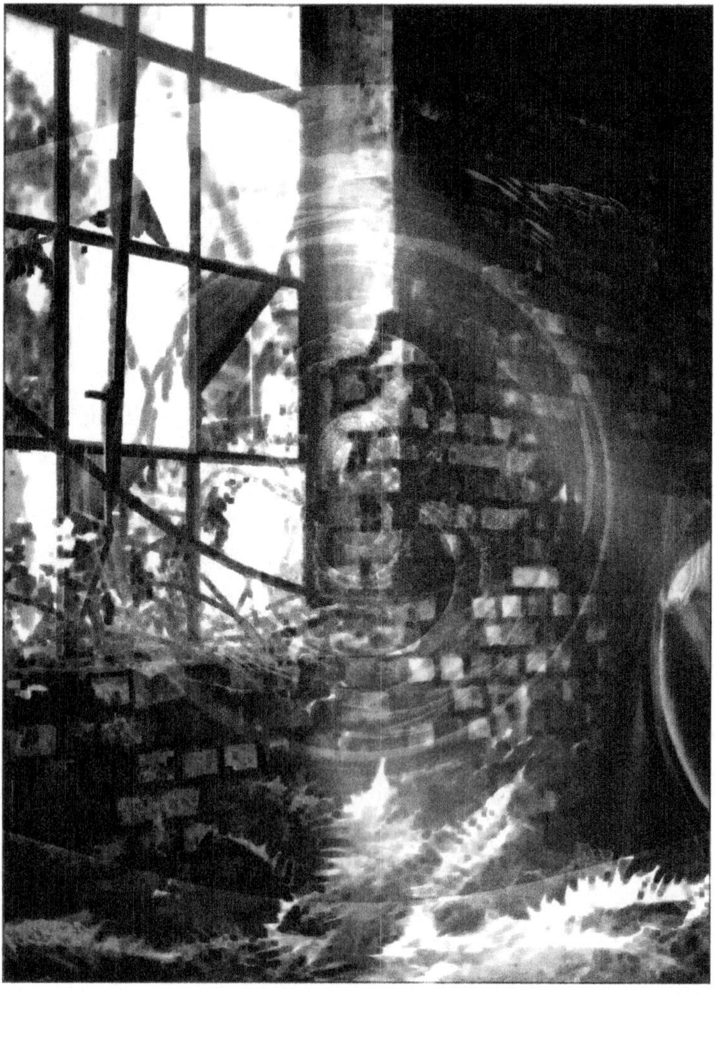

You'd smile, no doubt, to see me so broken,
I hunch over and heave as if I have anything left to give,
Instead of the expected result, a piercing noise breaks the silence,
A sound of sorrow for none to hear.

Agony, blood and tears,
Fists pounding unrelenting ground,
Bruises forming, feelings fading,
Rage consuming.

Oh gods, I miss you,
Your teasing tone,
The skin I never once felt,
Your charming enthral that leaves me shaking in terror.

My screaming morphs into begging,
My broken form on the ground,
Sobs wrecked my body without mercy,
I wish for you to return, to care.

But my begging isn't about you any more,
It's about what I'm feeling:
Useless, my world has splintered,
If you don't care you won't mind this wish of mine.

At last I crawl to the end of the road,
My lonely, fucked up road,
And I imagine I can see you sneering down at me,
You offer me your hand, I open my mouth:
"Kill me."

-

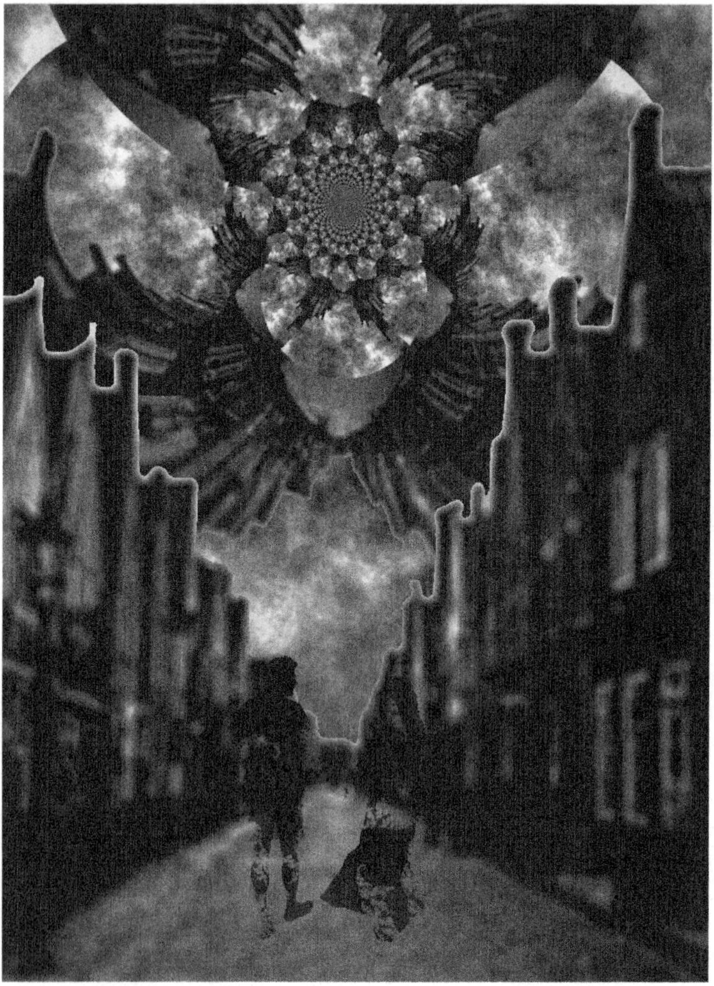

The Last Time

I think back to the last time I thought he was mine,
We walked side by side down a cobbled street,
We had dinner, and I put too much cheese on mine,
I remember the fond smile on his lips.

I remember later, when he told me he didn't want me,
And lips closed over mine,
I was desperate to believe he had changed his mind -
It was not so: she held me as I cried.

She held on, and I tried,
But the harder I held on the more I began to crumble,
Then numbness took over,
Suddenly, we were done.

That night I went to sleep,
No one else knew:
I felt my soul split and screamed silently,
Never had I felt such pain.

I wonder if they felt the same,
But the part of me that was theirs left me long ago,
I can only remember now that I loved them,
But that I was not enough.

-

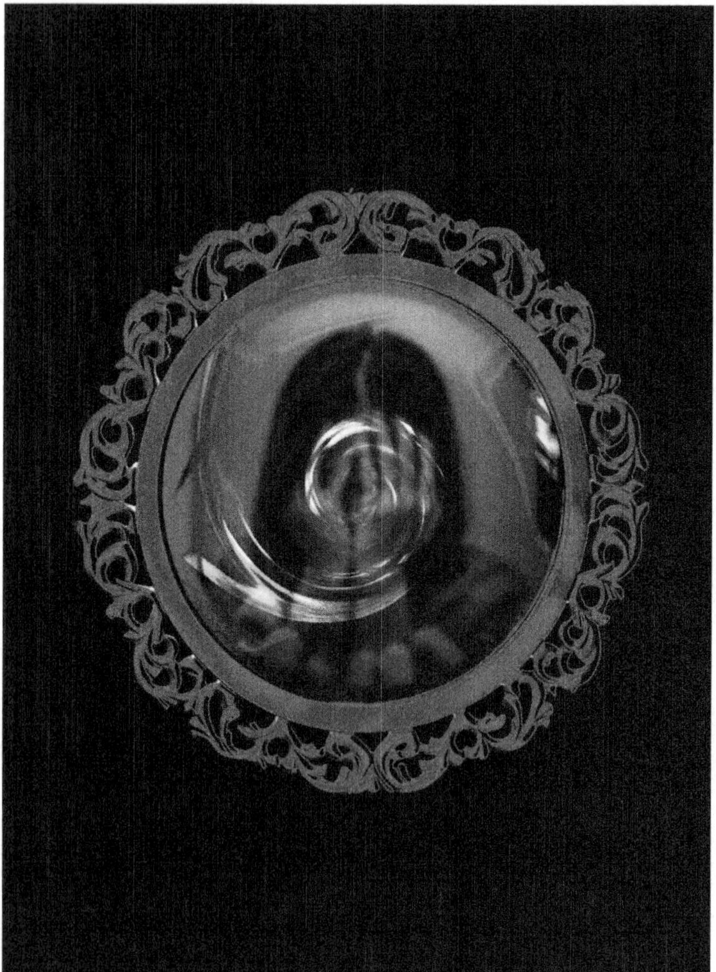

Just Scenes

There's a scene in my head,
But pen on paper doesn't pan out.

A familiar face and a smile,
Warm hands, warmer eyes.

Focus.
Just write.

The scene should play like any other,
But...? No, that wouldn't work.

Good intentions,
Hellish cuts.

A scene.
Dreadfully gruesome.

Writing flows with but a thought,
and drifting through words, I ponder:
The romance turning to horror -
Is my story a mirror?

-

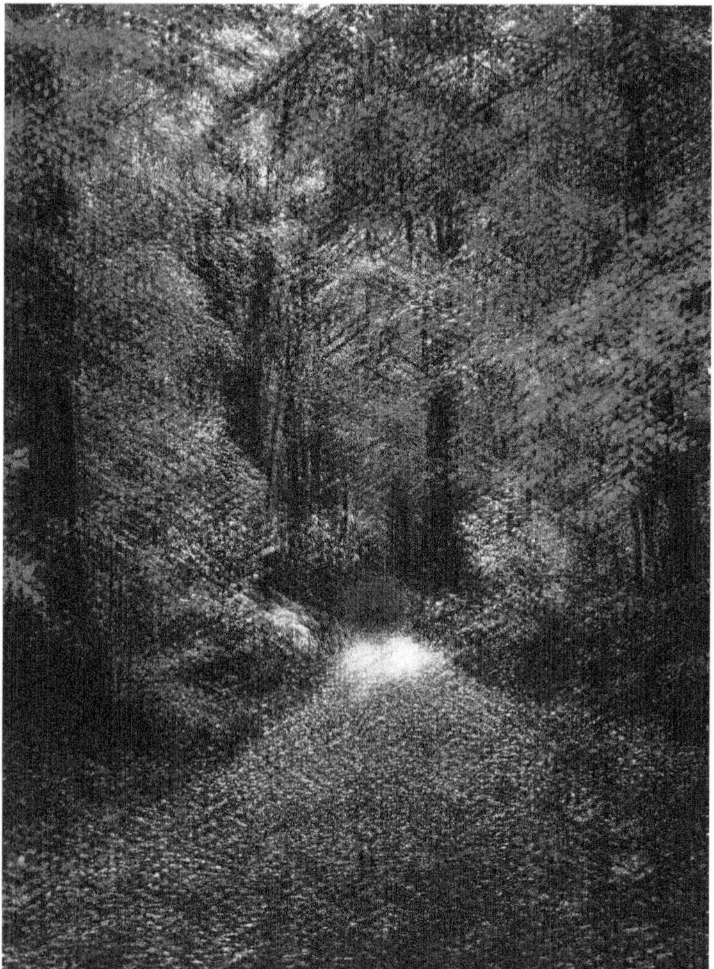

In Autumn

She loved the leaves,
The way they crunched beneath her feet,
She delighted in their changing colours,
And never laughed so freely than when wrapped up in her admiration of it.

Then - One night when her lips touched mine,
Her mouth was hot,
She burned against me as if she hoarded the sun's own passion,
I, mere kindling, was lost beneath her.

Yet hoped still she'd love me as one of her beloved trees,
Ready to Fall.

-

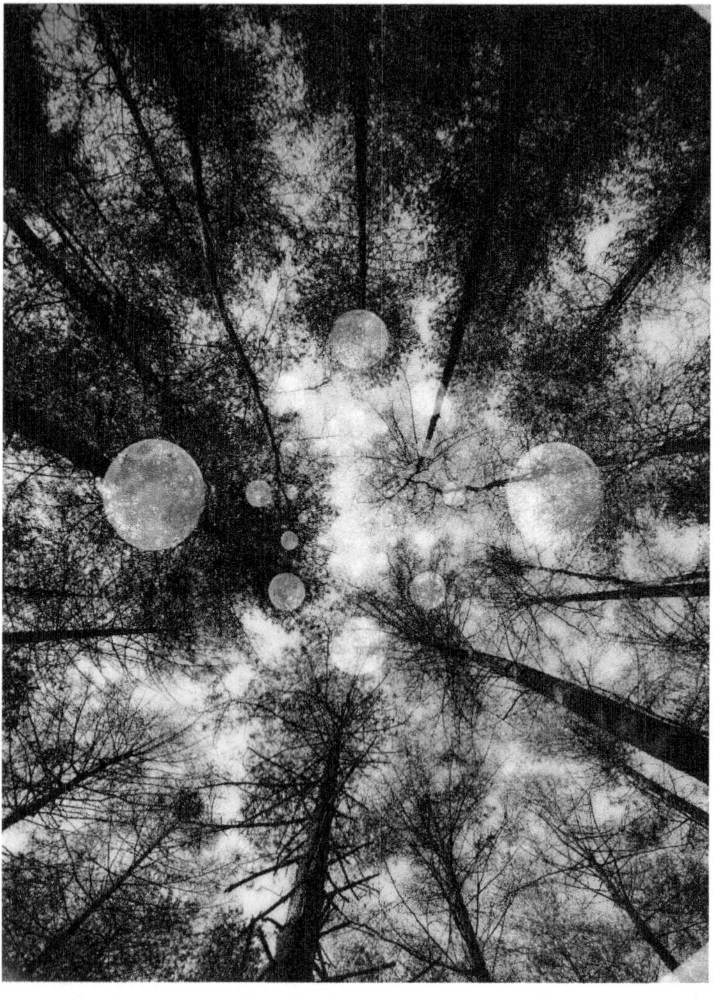

To Evoke

Your name in my mouth:
Scalding steel sliding through flesh,
Severed nerves and trembling legs,
A stopped heart.

Words that once came so easily are stunted,
Awkward even,
Jittery fingertips hovering over unpressed keys,
The backspace eroded,
It only un-does so much.

My name in your hand:
Fluttering and incandescent,
Pinned to the page until death,
Hauntingly studied, still beautiful.

The sin you make me feel.

-

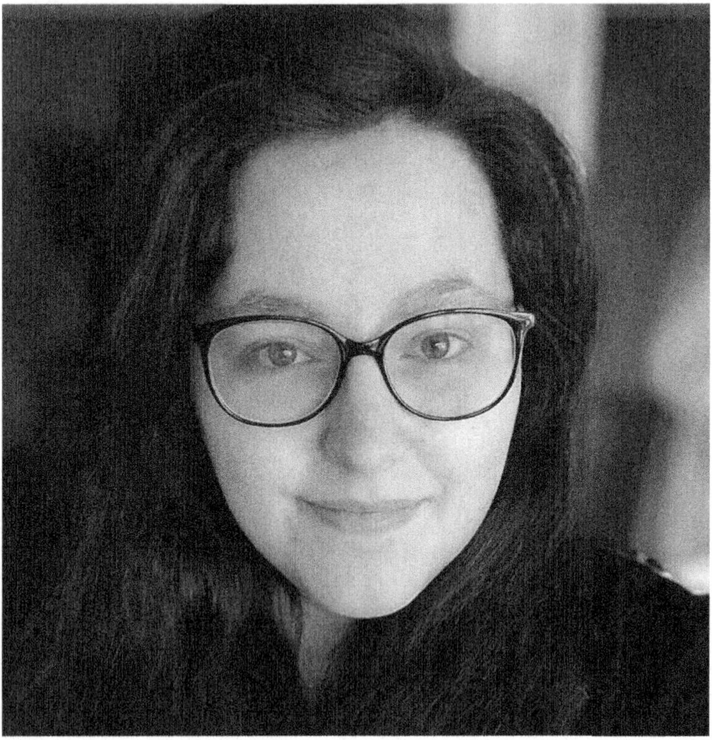

Connect with the Author

Thank you for taking the time to read my poetry. It took me a long time to get to the stage where I could put my work out there, so thank you for taking the time to absorb the words within these pages, and the artwork that accompanies each poem.

If you wish to connect with me, I am in the early stages of setting up author social media pages, so for now please feel free to send any queries or questions to the email address below, and take care!

cladams.official@gmail.com

Printed in Great Britain
by Amazon